Sandy's Incredible Shrinking Footprint

Written by
Femida Handy
and Carole Carpenter

Illustrated by
Adrianna Steele-Card

Second Story Press

Sandy skipped down the steps of her Grandpa's house. Her dog, Pepper, raced past her and bolted down the hill, heading for the beach and the wide blue sea. She stopped for a moment and took a big, deep breath of the fresh sea air. It was SUCH a perfect summer day!

Sandy and her parents lived in the city, but they visited Grandpa every summer. It was the best three weeks of the whole year. Pepper thought so too. By the time Sandy reached the seashore, he was running in all directions. Splashing in the waves, chasing seagulls, and rolling in the sand.

"No, Pepper! You'll get all dirty!"

The beach was Sandy's favorite place in the world. It was Grandpa's favorite place too, and he was teaching her all about it. He told her about sea animals like starfish and jellyfish and octopuses.

He showed her tiny crabs that skittered over the beach and buried themselves in the sand. He found perfect seashells for her, no bigger than her smallest fingernail, and showed her footprints made by different birds.

"Rooff! Rooff!"

Sandy looked over her shoulder to see what Pepper was barking at and — OW! — fell over some half-burned logs. Somebody had built a bonfire here, and she had landed right in their garbage. Yuck! What a mess!

Bits of hotdog buns, squished pop cans, empty popcorn bags, even a bright yellow plastic mustard container — who would leave such a pile of trash? Didn't they know about picking up after themselves? Hadn't they ever heard of recycling?

Sandy was disgusted. The beach was so beautiful. Nobody had the right to spoil it like this. She picked up a grubby plastic bag and put the mustard bottle and the pop cans in it for recycling.

"No, Pepper, don't eat those dirty old buns!"

She filled another bag with rubbish. Candy wrappers, chip bags – a dill pickle? Ick! Her hands were filthy and streaked with black from the burned logs. But she kept working. Nobody could do this to HER beach!

Suddenly a shadow loomed over Sandy. Somebody was right behind her. Somebody big. Somebody HUGE!

Oh, no! It's a MONSTER of garbage! Sandy had heard stories about a crazy old woman who roamed the beach picking up junk. She put it in bags and hung the bags all over herself, so she looked like a walking mountain of garbage.

What should Sandy do? Scream? Run away? And what about Pepper? Where was he?

"Oh my!" said the giant shadow.
"Let me help you with this mess."

Sandy gulped. Then she remembered what Grandpa had said about the Garbage Lady. "She's harmless and she's not crazy," he had told Sandy. "She's just...well...a little different."

The Garbage Lady bent to pick up a greasy paper bag. "Isn't this sad?" she said. "Imagine what the world would look like if everybody dumped their garbage and nobody cleaned up after themselves."

"There'd be PILES OF PAPER!" the Garbage Lady boomed.

"TOWERS OF TIN CANS!"

"PYRAMIDS OF PLASTIC!"

"STACKS OF STYROFOAM!"

Sandy picked up a wad of soggy paper napkins and looked up at the Garbage Lady. "I guess maybe these were once part of a tree." What a strange thought! "Maybe a tree far away. And it took land to grow that tree, and machines to make the napkins, too, and then trucks and trains to get them here. Does that mean I shouldn't use paper napkins? Or drink pop from cans?"

The Garbage Lady smiled. "It means you should think about your footprint."

Sandy looked down at her sneakers, puzzled – what was wrong with her footprints? The Garbage Lady laughed.

"Not the footprints you leave with your feet. The footprint of your life is the mark you leave on the world. Its size depends on what you eat...what you play with...how you get around...all kinds of little choices can make your footprint smaller. You can throw out a pop can, or recycle it – which one makes your footprint smaller?"

"Recycling, right?" said Sandy.

Pepper started barking, and Sandy heard her mom calling her. "I have to go home for lunch," she said. "It was great meeting you. Maybe I'll see you again!"

"I hope so, my dear. Take care. And don't forget about shrinking your footprint!" The Garbage Lady tied several more bags of junk to her belt and her backpack and then walked off down the beach.

Sandy picked up the last three bags and ran home, with Pepper leaping around her.

"I met the Garbage Lady, Mom! She's really nice! We cleaned up a big mess on the beach! Do you know about footprints?"

"Stop and take a breath!" said Sandy's mother. "You're quite a big mess yourself. You'd better go and wash up."

"I am going to shrink my footprint, Mom!" Sandy shouted as she bounded up the stairs.

Her mother looked puzzled.

Sandy chattered all through lunch about garbage and footprints. "I know we try to reuse stuff. We use brown paper bags to wrap things for mailing, and I use old egg cartons for storing my treasures," she said. "And we recycle a lot. But I want to make our footprints even smaller!"

"I know the first thing we can do," said Grandpa. "We can make a list." They all put their minds to work, and the list got longer and longer. The grown-ups thought of grown-up footprint-shrinking ideas, and Sandy added footprint-shrinking things that she could do.

Sandy smiled as she imagined her own footprint shrinking and shrinking. And then she got up and danced ever so gently around the room on her very small tippy toes.

Her footprint was getting tinier and tinier.

What about yours?

WAYS TO SHRINK OUR FOOTPRINTS

1. Walk or bike instead of driving the car.

2. Grow some of our own food...like herbs and tomatoes.

3. Buy more things made nearby, instead of things shipped from far away.

4. Give old clothes and toys to second-hand stores or have a garage sale.

5. Start a compost heap in the garden to turn garbage into nourishing soil.

6. Trade books with our friends or go to the library.

7. Write on both sides of each sheet of paper.

8. Turn off the lights when we leave a room.

9. Turn off the tap while brushing our teeth.

10. Take shorter showers.

11. Turn down the heat overnight.

12. Ask friends if they can think of making their footprints smaller too.

And do you know what? All the artwork in this book was made from recycled and natural materials!

Library and Archives Canada Cataloguing in Publication

Handy, Femida, 1949-
Sandy's incredible shrinking footprint / by Femida Handy and
Carole Carpenter ; illustrated by Adrianna Steele-Card.

ISBN 978-1-897187-69-2

1. Nature—Effect of human beings on—Juvenile fiction.
2. Recycling (Waste, etc.)—Juvenile fiction. 3. Environmental
protection—Juvenile fiction. I. Carpenter, Carole Henderson,
1944- II. Steele-Card, Adrianna, 1963- III. Title.

PS8615.A55295S26 2009   jC813'.6   C2009-906111-2

Edited by Gena K. Gorrell
Designed by Melissa Kaita

Second Story Press gratefully acknowledges the support of the
Ontario Arts Council and the Canada Council for the Arts for our
publishing program. We acknowledge the financial support of
the Government of Canada through the Book Publishing Industry
Development Program.

Printed and bound in China

ONTARIO ARTS COUNCIL
CONSEIL DES ARTS DE L'ONTARIO

Canada Council   Conseil des Arts
for the Arts   du Canada

Published by
SECOND STORY PRESS
20 Maud Street, Suite 401
Toronto, Ontario, Canada
M5V 2M5
www.secondstorypress.ca

FSC
Mixed Sources
Product group from well-managed
forests and other controlled sources
Cert no. BV-COC-874701
www.fsc.org
© 1996 Forest Stewardship Council

*For our children and
their children*
– Femida Handy and
Carole Carpenter

*For all the children
and animals who
inherit this earth*
– Adrianna Steele-Card